Stand in My Shoes

Kids Learning About Empathy

Written by Bob Sornson
and Illustrated by Shelley Johannes

2207 Jackson Street
Golden, Colorado 80401-2300
www.loveandlogic.com
800-338-4065

Stand in My Shoes: Kids Learning About Empathy

Summary: After Emily asks her big sister what the word "empathy" means, Emily decides to pay closer attention to others during her day.

Library of Congress Cataloging-in-Publication Data
Sornson, Bob
Stand in My Shoes: Kids Learning About Empathy/Bob Sornson–First Edition
ISBN-13: 978-1-935326-45-8
1. Elementary school. 2. Empathy. 3. Emotions and feelings.
I. Sornson, Bob II. Title
Library of Congress Control Number: 2012953816

Illustrations created with pencil and digital paint by Shelley Johannes
Layout and cover design by Jacqueline L. Challiss Hill
Project Coordination by Nelson Publishing & Marketing/Ferne Press
Ferne Press is an imprint of Nelson Publishing & Marketing
366 Welch Road, Northville, MI 48167
www.nelsonpublishingandmarketing.com
(248) 735-0418

Dedication

For decades he has delivered the same consistent message: set firm limits in a loving way, let children make decisions sometimes, allow them to struggle, allow them to solve the problems they create whenever possible, let them learn from their mistakes. Simple wisdom, needed now more than ever in our lives.

Throughout his years of training parents and teachers, his message has been built upon a foundation of empathy and respect for the children who come into our lives. Love these beautiful children. Help them grow strong. This book is dedicated to Jim Fay, one of the great teachers.

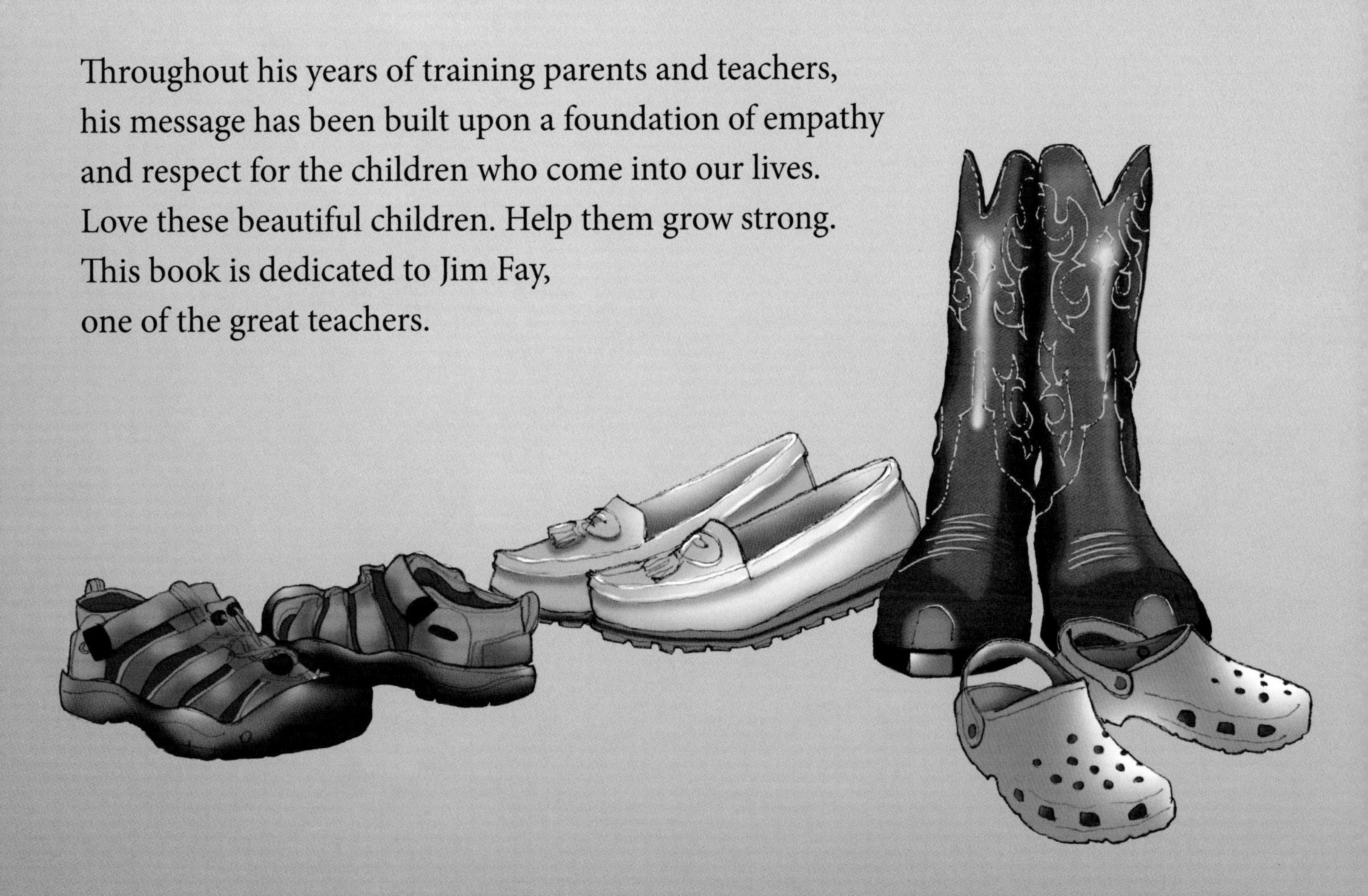

"Emily! This is the fourth time you've barged into my room. I am trying to study for a big test."

"I just want to talk to you," Emily whined.

Alicia closed her book and said,

"Can't you have a

little empathy?"

Emily had no idea what her big sister meant. "What's empathy?"

"Empathy is when you understand how someone is feeling because you imagine what it's like to be them or stand in their shoes. People are grateful when you notice how they feel. I'm worried about my test, and I'd really appreciate it if you'd scram so I can study."

Emily was grumpy as she left her sister's room, but she thought about Alicia's words.

Would people really appreciate it if she noticed how they felt?

The next morning, Emily went to the kitchen for breakfast. Her dad was making coffee and had spilled some coffee grounds. He didn't look very happy.

"Dad, are you in a hurry?" she asked.

"Yes, sweetie. I have a big presentation at work and need to get going."

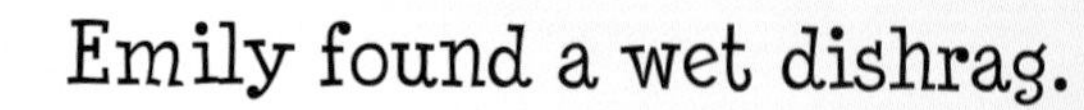

Emily found a wet dishrag.

"You look tired, Dad. How about if I clean up the coffee while you get your other stuff together?

Would that help?"

For a moment, Emily's
dad just looked at her.
Then he hugged her.

"You are the best, Em,"
he said as he grabbed
his coat and hurried
out the back door.

It was drizzling outside as Emily waited for the school bus. As it pulled up, one of the older kids accidentally knocked into a little girl as she was getting onto the bus. Rosie lost her balance and sat down hard on the wet cement.

"Hey!" yelled Emily.

"Watch out for the little kids."

Then Emily turned
to the little girl. “Well, that’s a
yucky way to start the day.”

“I’m okay,” Rosie replied.
But she struggled with her
heavy backpack.

Emily took Rosie’s hand and
pulled her up, then
helped her onto the bus.

In class, Mrs. Fitch was not her usual laughing self.

After the morning writing lesson, Mrs. Fitch went back to her desk instead of walking around the classroom like she usually did. Emily noticed that her teacher's eyes were red and that she wiped her nose on a tissue.

"Mrs. Fitch, is there something wrong?"

"My little dog, Buster, died last night," she said quietly. "He was very sick. We were hoping he'd get better, but he didn't."

"Oh, no," said Emily. "I'm not sure how you feel, but it has to hurt."

"It does.
Thank you
for asking."

In the cafeteria, she noticed Mrs. Wattles struggling to lift a tray of steamed vegetables into its place on the serving line.

"That sure looks heavy," Emily said.

"It is!" Mrs. Wattles said. "I get a workout every day when I serve lunch."

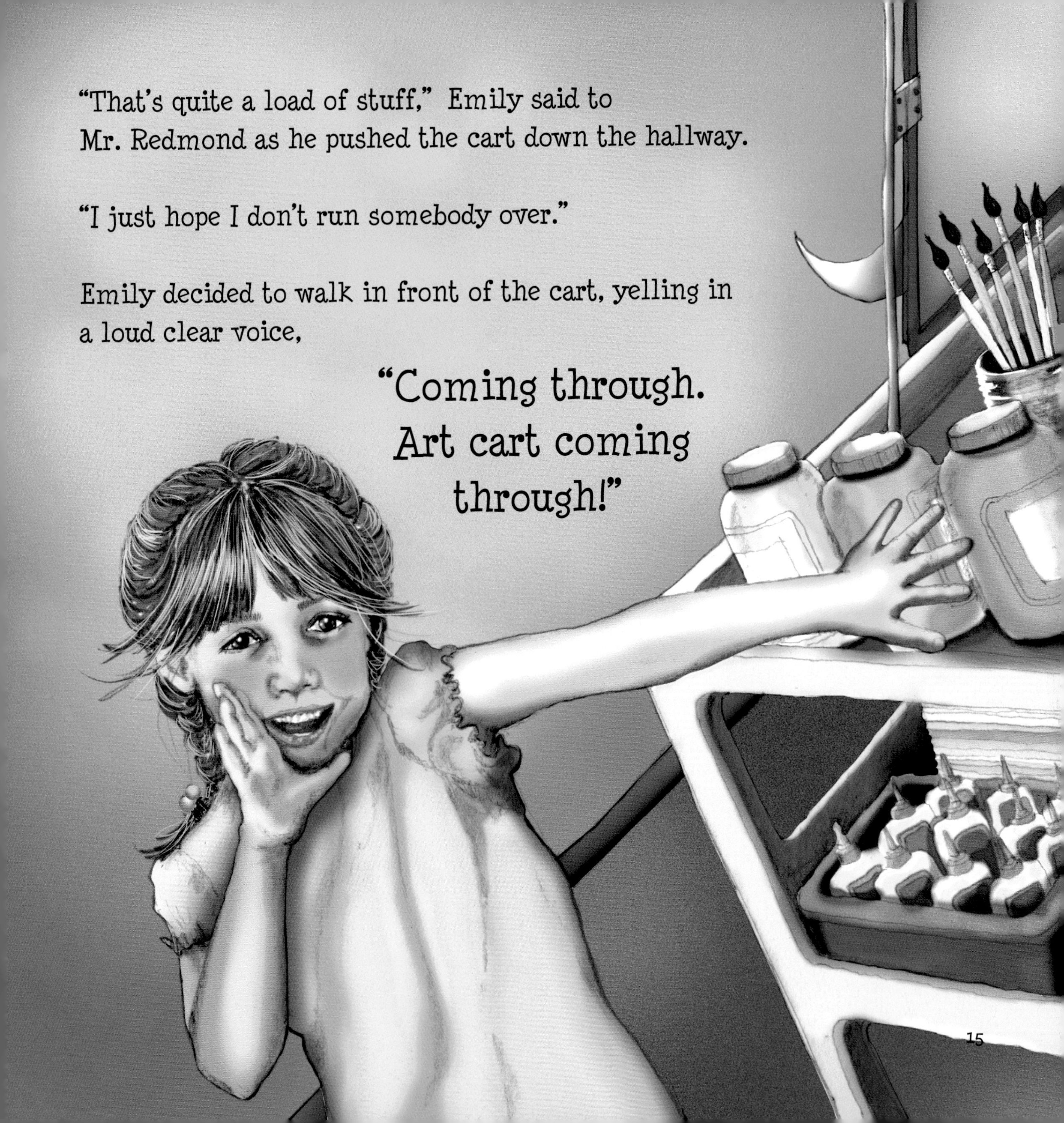

"That's quite a load of stuff," Emily said to Mr. Redmond as he pushed the cart down the hallway.

"I just hope I don't run somebody over."

Emily decided to walk in front of the cart, yelling in a loud clear voice,

"Coming through. Art cart coming through!"

"Get outta my way!" Tommy said as he pushed Samantha, Emily's friend, out of the line. "It's my turn!"

Tommy did this a lot at recess.

"Tommy! How'd you like it if I pushed you out of line when you were waiting your turn?"

"Probably not good," Tommy replied. "I love the tire swing."

"Samantha loves it as much as you do,
so don't push her and try to take cuts, okay?"

"Sorry," mumbled Tommy as he walked to the end of the line.

After school, Mr. Peterson said, "Hello, Emily. I hope you had a wonderful day."

She stopped and looked at him. "I did have a wonderful day. But Mr. Peterson, every day you say something nice to me.

You never forget!"

As she walked to her seat, Emily could hear Mr. Peterson greet each child as they got on the bus. She sat down next to Samantha.

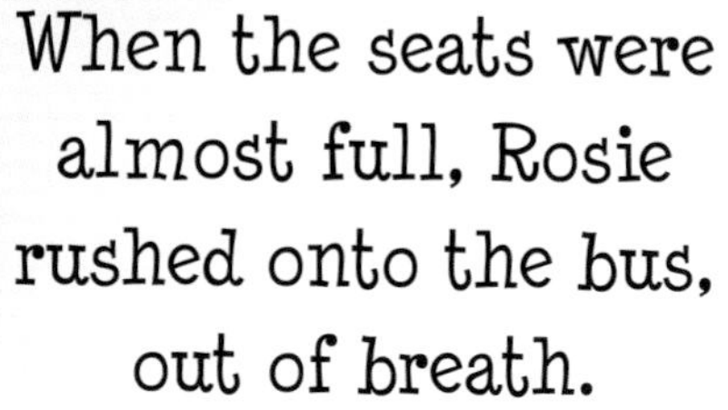

When the seats were almost full, Rosie rushed onto the bus, out of breath.

"Oh, no! There isn't a place for me."

Emily nudged Samantha and then asked her to slide over.

"Rosie, you can sit with us."

"I can? Thanks!"

When Emily got home, her mom asked,
"How was your day, Em?
You look deep in thought."

"I'm fine, but I'm wondering about
something."

"What's that?"

"You always seem to
notice how I'm feeling."

"Part of being a mom."

"But how about you?
Who notices how
you're feeling?"
asked Emily.

"Wow, Em," said her mom. "That's a very thoughtful question. I guess the answer is Aunt Carla, and my friends Nancy and Shawna, and mostly your dad. Sometimes Alicia, and now you.

Why do you ask?"

"Just wondering," said Emily. "I'm starving.
Is there anything good for a snack?"

"Let's make something together."

It was almost bedtime. Emily could see Alicia studying in her room. Instead of barging in, Emily knocked on the door.

"Can I come in, or are you busy?"

“You look like you want to talk,” said Alicia. “Come on in.”

“I’ve been noticing how people feel,” Emily said. “You know, that empathy stuff.”

“So what happened? What did you learn?”

"People really like it when you recognize how they feel. Just noticing seems to touch their hearts."

"You got it, Em!"

"But there's something more.
When I care enough to notice how others feel,

something changes inside of me,"

Emily explained.

"It sounds like you enjoy that feeling."

"Yes, I do," replied Emily.

"Good. Now get outta here so I can study!"

Letter to Reader

Dear Reader,

Empathy is the heart of Love and Logic. The practice of understanding how another person is feeling keeps us from becoming that angry parent or teacher. Empathy is part of a strong, positive emotional state in which we can treat others with respect while still setting appropriate limits on how others behave around us. It gives us that glimpse into the heart of another person and helps us remember to always put the "love" into Love and Logic.

Empathy does not offer excuses for bad choices. As a parent or teacher, sometimes empathy must be followed by a consequence or by allowing some sadness to come into the lives of our children. But with empathy, we can give consequences with love rather than anger. Empathy is the foundation of all emotional intelligence. By helping our children learn empathy, we raise the odds they will have strong, positive social relationships, truly care for others, and be able to set appropriate limits in their own lives without using angry behaviors or words.

Sincerely,

Bob Sornson

Author & Illustrator

Bob Sornson, PhD, was a classroom teacher and school administrator for over thirty years and is the founder of the Early Learning Foundation. He is dedicated to helping schools and parents give every child an opportunity to achieve early learning success. His pre-K to grade 3 Early Learning Success Initiative has demonstrated that we can help many more children become successful learners for life.

Bob is the author of numerous articles, books, and audio recordings. *Fanatically Formative, Successful Learning During the Crucial K-3 Years* (Corwin, 2012), *Creating Classrooms Where Teachers Love to Teach* (Love and Logic Press, 2005), and *The Juice Box Bully* (Ferne Press, 2010) are among his best-sellers. Bob is also the author of the Stand Up/Speak Up Program (www.no-bystanders.com), teaching children to make the choices to stand up and speak up for themselves and others. To contact Bob or learn more about his publications and workshops, please visit www.earlylearningfoundation.com.

Shelley Johannes began her artistic career after ten years in the architectural design industry. While that was fun, she found her dream job when motherhood introduced her to the world of children's books. Five years and a dozen books later, she still pinches herself everyday. A library fanatic who used to walk to the bus stop with her nose in a book, Shelley still reads every chance she gets. Iced cappuccinos and book recommendations are her favorite gifts. When she's not painting or playing with her boys, she writes about her adventures in books at thebookdiariesblog.com. Shelley wishes she could live in perpetual autumn, but for now she lives in Michigan where she enjoys the colorful chaos of life, with her husband, Bob, and their two boys, Matthew and Nolan.